19153

MW00962886

SMART
STRUCTURES

TUNNELS

Julie Richards

A⁺

This edition first published in 2004 in the United States of America by
Smart Apple Media.

Smart Apple Media
1980 Lookout Drive
North Mankato
Minnesota 56003

Library of Congress Cataloging-in-Publication Data

Richards, Julie.
　Tunnels / by Julie Richards.
　p. cm. — (Smart structures)
　Summary: Describes various kinds of tunnels, the methods and materials of their
　construction, and amazing or disastrous examples.
　ISBN 1-58340-346-9
　1. Tunnels—Design and construction—Juvenile literature. [1. Tunnels—Design and
　construction.] I. Title.
　TA807.R525 2003
　624.1'93—dc21　　　　　　　　　　　　　　　　　　　2002044629

First Edition
9 8 7 6 5 4 3 2 1

First published in 2003 by
MACMILLAN EDUCATION AUSTRALIA PTY LTD
627 Chapel Street, South Yarra, Australia 3141

Associated companies and representatives throughout the world.

Edited by Anna Fern
Text design by Cristina Neri, Canary Graphic Design
Cover design by Cristina Neri, Canary Graphic Design
Layout by Nina Sanadze
Illustrations by Margaret Hastie, IKON Computergraphics
Photo research by Legend Images

Printed in Thailand

Acknowledgements
The author and the publisher are grateful to the following for permission to reproduce
copyright material:

Cover photograph: view through a road tunnel, courtesy of Getty Images.

Australian Picture Library/Corbis, pp. 12, 22, 28, 29; Digital Vision, p. 5 (bottom left);
Eurotunnel, pp. 5 (bottom right), 24; Eye Ubiquitous, p. 5 (top left); Getty Images,
pp. 1, 4, 5 (top right), 9, 13, 14, 18 (top), 19, 20, 21, 23; Mary Evans Picture Library, p. 26;
Brian Parker, p. 25; Photolibrary.com, pp. 7 (bottom), 18 (bottom); QA Photos, pp. 8, 10,
16; Reuters, pp. 11, 27; Smithsonian Institution, p. 7 (top); Southern California LEGO Train
Club, design by Paul Thomas, Riverside, California, photo by Thomas Michon, Irvine,
California, p. 30.

While every care has been taken to trace and acknowledge copyright, the publisher tenders
their apologies for any accidental infringement where copyright has proved untraceable.
Where the attempt has been unsuccessful, the publisher welcomes information that would
redress the situation.

CONTENTS

KEY WORDS

When a word is printed in **bold** you can look up its meaning
in the key words box on the same page. You can also look
up the meaning of words in the glossary on page 31.

TUNNELS AS STRUCTURES

A **structure** is made up of many different parts joined together. The shapes of the parts and the way they are joined together help a structure to stand up and do the job for which it has been designed. The **materials** used to make a structure can be made stronger or weaker, depending on their shape and how they are put together.

Tunnels are made by humans, but animals and insects also make them. Other natural tunnels are made by underground streams slowly wearing away the rocks beneath the soil. People build tunnels to help them move from one place to another. Tunnels are used to:

- cross natural obstacles such as mountains, rivers, and narrow strips of sea
- allow people and wildlife to cross beneath a major road or railroad safely and easily
- carry traffic around major cities rather than through them, therefore easing traffic jams and pollution
- move trains under a city without taking up expensive land on the surface that could be used for housing, stores, and offices
- carry services such as electricity, communications cables, drinking water, and wastewater
- find and mine minerals and precious metals
- escape in an emergency.

Termites tunneling into wood ▼

KEY WORDS

structure something that is made up of many parts joined together

materials anything used to make a structure

termites ant-like insects

Types of tunnels

Humans make many different types of tunnels. Not all tunnels are built the same way. How a tunnel is built depends on:

- what it is needed for
- the place where it is to be built
- the type of ground to be tunneled through.

This tunnel carries road traffic through very high mountains. The tunnel makes the journey much shorter, safer, and easier.

This tunnel, built by the ancient Romans in the first century A.D., carried wastewater away from cities to help keep them clean and free of disease.

This tunnel is very deep. Miners are digging out coal and sending it to the surface to be cleaned and sorted.

The Channel Tunnel carries trains across the English Channel, between England and France. Before the tunnel was built, people crossed by ferry, hovercraft, or airplane. The journey was longer, more expensive, and sometimes uncomfortable.

LOOKING AT TUNNELS

If you look closely at a tunnel, you will notice:

- the different parts which have been joined together to make the tunnel
- the shapes of these parts.

Tunnels have to carry extremely heavy loads. Earthquakes, landslides, and underground water can make a tunnel collapse. It is important that the tunnel is made from the right shapes joined together in the right way so that it is safe.

Tunnel shapes

Rectangles, arches, and triangles are the strongest shapes used to build big structures, but they all have their breaking point.

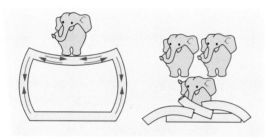

Rectangle

One elephant on a rectangle makes the top side bend. The weight of three elephants causes the top side to break.

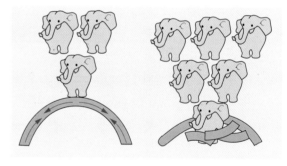

Arch

The weight of three elephants on an arch spreads along the curve to the ground below. The weight of six elephants causes the sides to spread apart and collapse.

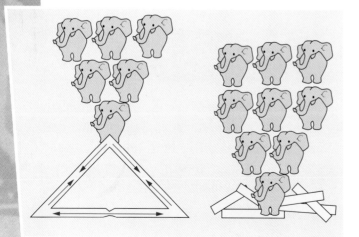

Triangle

The weight of six elephants on a triangle causes the two top sides to squeeze together and the bottom side to pull apart. The triangle is the strongest shape, but a herd of elephants makes the bottom side stretch so much that it snaps in half.

Arches

A tunnel is a structure built around a hole called a bore. If you look at the entrance to a long road or railroad tunnel, you will usually see that it is arch shaped. All deep tunnels have an arched roof, because it is a very strong shape. An arch carries the massive weight of the soil and rock above the tunnel, spreading the weight outwards onto the sides of the tunnel.

How do you make an arch?

The Romans were famous for their strong stone arches, which they began to use more than 2,000 years ago. They built their arches around wooden frames. When the final stone was placed at the top of the center of the arch, the frame was taken away. The center top stone, called the keystone, pressed on all the other stones. Arches can stay up even without any **cement** between the stones.

▲ A wooden frame holds up the arch entrance of the Hoosac Tunnel, built between 1851 and 1873, in Massachusetts.

Triangles

Triangles are the strongest, stiffest, and most stable of all the shapes. Rectangles can be strengthened by fixing extra supports to make them into a triangle. This is called **bracing**.

Some wooden bridges are protected from harsh weather by having a shelter built over them. These are called covered bridges. Covered bridges, **avalanche shelters**, and **lava shelters** are also tunnels. Their structure is easier to see because these tunnels are above ground. A covered bridge will often use triangles and braced rectangles in its walls and supports to make it stable, especially if it is wooden. It does not have to support the weight of tons of rock and soil pushing against it like an underground tunnel does, but it must be able to withstand strong winds and the vibration of a moving train. Avalanche and lava shelters are usually arched or curved so that they do not collapse when snow or lava covers them.

▲ The walls of this tunnel have been braced and made into triangles.

KEY WORDS

cement an ingredient in concrete which makes the concrete harden like stone

bracing something fastened to an object to keep it stiff and straight, just like the braces worn on teeth

avalanche shelters tunnels that protect a mountain road or railroad from being buried beneath moving snow and ice

lava shelters tunnels that people can escape through when a nearby volcano erupts

THE PARTS OF A TUNNEL

All tunnels must have their walls and roofs supported by linings. Without linings, a tunnel cannot safely do the job it has been designed for. A tunnel also needs **temporary** supports as it is built.

Supports and linings

Rock and soil can fall from the roof and walls of an unsupported tunnel. This slows the tunnelers down and can be very dangerous. If the tunnel passes through soft ground, soil can slip away from the foundations of nearby buildings, damaging their structure and even making them unsafe.

The tunnel roof and walls need to be supported by a concrete tunnel lining. The lining keeps any soil and loose rock in place and stops the ground above the tunnel from slipping. Tunnel linings also waterproof the tunnel and prevent water from underground streams, burst water pipes, or rivers above the tunnel from leaking into it.

◄ A piece of tunnel lining is placed against the tunnel wall.

Tunnel lining

Cut-and-cover tunnels and underwater tube tunnels are known as ready-made tunnels. These tunnels are built from above ground rather than tunneling through the ground. Cut-and-cover tunnels are usually quite shallow.
The linings and other parts of these tunnels are normally made in a factory, brought to the tunneling site, and fitted when they are needed.

Fresh air

The deeper a tunnel goes, the hotter it becomes. With a lot of machinery working in such a narrow space, the exhaust fumes and heat from their engines soon make it very uncomfortable. Dust and, sometimes, poisonous gases are released when rock is broken apart. All this makes tunneling a very dangerous job. Fresh air, or ventilation, is extremely important.

Natural ventilation

Tunneling animals such as the **prairie dog** build very long tunnels with good ventilation. The tunnels have an entrance at each end. One end opens onto flat ground. The other forms a chimney which is built up about 11 inches (30 cm) above the ground. Warm, stale air rises to the top of the chimney. As it is drawn out, cooler fresh air is sucked in at the other end.

Early ventilation

Early tunnelers copied the natural tunnel builders by digging **shafts** that rose from the tunnel floor to short chimneys above the ground. They lit fires in **braziers** on the tunnel floor beneath these shafts. As the hot air rose into the shaft, cooler air was dragged in from another opening in the tunnel. This helped keep the air moving and cooled the tunnel.

In 1837, heat from braziers helped to draw fresh air into this tunnel. ▶

In a modern tunnel, shafts are still dug down from the surface to the tunnel, but huge fans are now used to draw out hot, stale air and pump in fresh, cool air through pipes called ducts. Tunnelers also wear masks over their mouths and noses to prevent them from breathing in dust and fumes.

KEY WORDS

prairie dog a small, furry animal like a ground squirrel or possum which lives underground in large groups

shafts vertical passages or tunnels

braziers metal containers in which a fire can be burned

9

The first tunnels were lined with bricks or wood. Sometimes, tree trunks were used to prop up a tunnel. However, wood rotted quickly and the bricks would peel away from the walls. It was not unusual for tunnels of the past to collapse or flood. Some ancient tunnels were carved through solid rock. It was extremely hard work, but the rock made a strong lining. Today, the most important materials for building modern tunnels are steel and **concrete**.

▲ Tunneling machinery is lowered into a tunnel by a crane.

Concrete

Concrete is cheap, extremely strong, and can be made into any shape. Concrete is a mixture of cement, water, sand, and gravel. The wet, runny mixture is poured into wooden or metal molds so that it can harden into the right shape. Concrete dries to become as strong and hard as rock. A mug-sized piece of concrete can support a 33-ton (30-t) truck!

Shotcrete

Shotcrete is special sticky concrete that can be sprayed onto curved surfaces, such as tunnel walls and roofs, where it sets without running off. Shotcrete does not need to be poured into molds or tipped out of gigantic buckets. It is ideal for use in a cramped place such as a tunnel.

KEY WORDS

concrete a building material made by mixing cement and sand or gravel with water

Steel

Steel is an **alloy** made mostly of iron. Steel is used to make tunnel linings and temporary supports for tunnel walls and roofs. The steel must be coated with another metal called zinc or a layer of plastic. This protects the steel from water and stops it from rusting.

Concrete is only strong when you try to squash it. If you try to stretch it, concrete cracks quite easily. Steel is extremely strong when it is stretched. Pouring wet concrete over bunches of steel wires or a mesh of steel bars strengthens the concrete and stops it from cracking as it stretches. This **reinforced** concrete is used in many large structures, especially in the parts that will be stretched.

▲ Can you see the steel bars sticking out from the reinforced concrete at this tunnel building site?

Future materials

Engineers are busy developing lighter, stronger materials from which tunnel linings can be built. In the future, there may be a new type of concrete made with an ingredient other than cement. The new concrete would harden in minutes so that tunnelers could work more quickly. Normal concrete can take a month or more to reach its full strength as it hardens.

KEY WORDS

alloy a mixture of two or more metals
reinforced made stronger
engineers people who design and build large structures

TUNNEL DESIGN

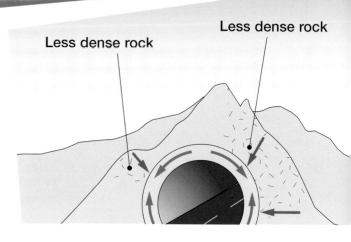

Less dense rock

Less dense rock

There are four types of tunnels:
- rock
- soft-ground
- cut-and-cover
- immersed-tube.

Rock tunnels

Rock tunnels are built through solid bedrock. Bedrock is a hard rock that reaches deep into Earth. In hills and mountains, bedrock is usually close to the surface, but in valleys it is covered by layers of sand, mud, or clay. Rock tunnels normally carry railroads, roads, and **canals** through hills and mountains. They can also be used to carry water beneath cities that are built on bedrock. Rock tunnels need little or no extra support while they are being built, because the rock walls are very thick. Some sections of the rock will be thinner than other sections.

This is a cross-section of a rock tunnel. Loose chunks of rock press on the side of the tunnel.

Hoosac Tunnel

The Hoosac Tunnel, in Massachusetts, was an early rock tunnel built between 1851 and 1873. More than two million tons of rock were carved out of the mountain range, using drills and dangerous explosives such as gunpowder and nitroglycerine. The process was slow, as each blast only produced a few feet of shattered rock. Twenty million bricks were used to line the 4.75-mile-long (7.6-km) tunnel.

◀ A rock tunnel in Utah

KEY WORDS

canals waterways made by humans

Soft-ground tunnels

Soft-ground tunnels are built through soft, crumbly rocks, clay, or mud. This type of ground is not as hard as solid rock, so there is no need to use explosives.

But soft ground can have its own problems. It is made up of loose grains of sandy soil and chunks of rock, which need to be supported during tunneling to prevent cave-ins. Soft ground is often waterlogged because some rocks are filled with tiny holes like sponges and the water seeps into them. Flooding is common in this type of tunnel, so special care needs to be taken. The wet, heavy ground pushes on all sides of the tunnel, squeezing its walls together.

Soft-ground tunnels are not as deep as rock tunnels. They are often used as pedestrian tunnels, water-supply systems, **sewers**, and for underground roads and rail systems.

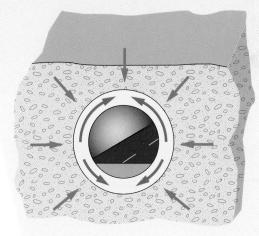

This is a cross-section of a soft-ground tunnel. The heavy, wet ground presses on all sides of the tunnel.

The Big Dig

The Central Artery/Tunnel Project, in Massachusetts, is known as the Big Dig. By the time it is completed, in 2004, this huge roadway tunnel will be eight lanes wide, 3.5 miles (5.6 km) long, and completely buried beneath dozens of skyscrapers. Special machines called clamshell excavators are being used to dig 120 feet (36.5 m) to reach the bedrock. To stop the soft ground from slipping and causing railroad tracks to collapse, engineers froze the ground. Hundreds of pipes were driven into the ground and filled with icy water. A road-digging machine then dug out the frozen soil. The machine has a moveable arm that grinds away the frozen soil, which is collected in a bucket and lifted out of the tunnel by a crane.

▼ The Big Dig

KEY WORDS

sewers channels that carry sewage to where it can be treated

Cut-and-cover tunnels

A cut-and-cover tunnel is dug from above ground rather than tunneling through it. Most cut-and-cover tunnels are not very deep. A trench is dug and all the soil and rocks are moved to one side. The walls and the roof of the tunnel are built from bricks, stones, or concrete. Often, the concrete tunnel parts arrive already made and the tunnel is constructed by placing the parts in the trench and joining them together. Once the tunnel is finished, it is covered with the soil and rocks that were dug out.

Cut-and-cover tunnels are quite fast and easy to build, and the land on top of them can be used for roadways, farmland, or buildings. They can be constructed alongside roads without causing too many problems for pedestrians and traffic. This type of tunnel is popular for pedestrian and traffic tunnels and for carrying services such as water, gas, electricity, and communications.

This is a cross-section of a cut-and-cover tunnel. This tunnel is pressed on from all sides, especially the top.

▼ The London Underground rail system in the 1800s

A famous cut-and-cover tunnel

The first part of the London Underground rail system was dug as a cut-and-cover tunnel in 1863. The tunnel system was designed to follow the streets above it. So, the tunnelers simply dug huge trenches in the streets they wanted to follow, lined the trenches with bricks, covered the trenches with arch roofs, and then put the street back on top. It created terrible problems, but, when completed, was a great success. The new rail system carried more than nine million people in its first year.

Immersed-tube tunnels

An immersed-tube tunnel is designed to carry roads and railroads under a river or a narrow strip of sea. These tunnels are quite tricky to build, as the water must be held back while the tunnel is being constructed. In the past, underwater tunnel builders used special **excavation** chambers to prevent water from gushing into them. Today, most underwater tunnels are ready-made tubes which are brought to where they are needed and connected to other tunnel sections already in place. Underwater tunnels have to be very strong because the water squeezes their walls. The deeper the water is, the harder it squeezes.

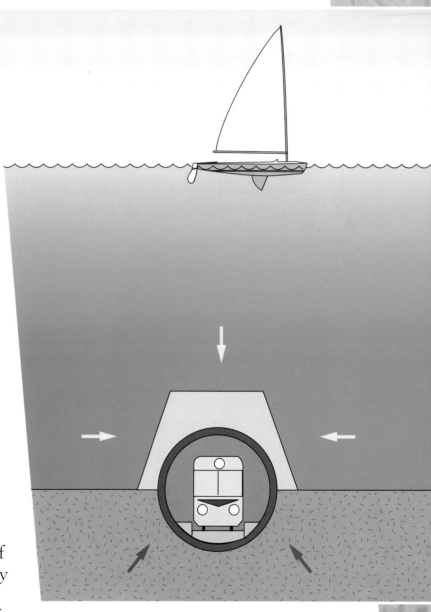

This is a cross-section of an immersed-tube tunnel. Water presses on all sides of the tunnel.

The Channel Tunnel

The Channel Tunnel is probably the most famous underwater tunnel in the world. It is a 32-mile (51-km) rail tunnel beneath the English Channel, linking England and France. The tunnel was dug from both ends at once. Four years later, both teams met in the middle, hundreds of feet beneath the sea.

Choosing the right tunnel design

Geologists measure the amount of water in the ground and test samples of rock and soil to discover if there are any weaknesses. Engineers work out the route for the tunnel and check to see if there are any buildings or important pipes that might be in the way.

It is important to keep the width of the tunnel as small as possible. The larger the tunnel's width, the greater the pushing and squeezing forces of the ground around it and the stronger the tunnel will need to be.

KEY WORDS

excavation digging
geologists scientists who study soil and rocks

BUILDING TUNNELS

Building a large tunnel is an enormous job that can take hundreds of people several years to finish. It is hot, dark, and dangerous work.

Going underground

Most tunnels are dug from both ends at once, but some tunnels are dug outwards from the middle. Shafts are always dug along the tunnel route. They are used to let fresh air into the tunnel and to remove the soil and rocks as the tunnel grows. Cranes lower the tunnel-digging machinery, tunnel linings, and temporary supports into the shaft closest to where they are needed. The shaft for lowering machinery into the Channel Tunnel was 180 feet (55 m) across and 246 feet (75 m) deep. The digging machines were so big that they could only be lowered into the tunnel in parts. Once inside, they had to be put together like a model kit.

KEY WORDS

hydraulic works by using water or another liquid under pressure

This is one of the massive moles used to bore the Channel Tunnel. It weighs nearly 1,103 tons (1,000 t) and is twice the length of a soccer field. Can you see the teeth on the cutting head?

Digging machines

Powerful digging machines do most of the hard excavating work. Different tunnels need different types of digging machines. Tunnel-boring machines (T.B.M.s) are called moles. A T.B.M. has large, sharp teeth on a giant spinning cutting head. It chews away at the ground in front of it. Other digging equipment includes smaller drills or a bigger drill that is pushed along a track by **hydraulic** jacks. In a rock tunnel, the rock may need to be shattered by explosives before any digging can begin.

Building soft-ground tunnels

A tunnel-boring machine is like a long metal tube. It is used to bore through soft rocks to make soft-ground tunnels. The **tunnel face**, roof, and walls must be supported to stop them from caving in behind the machine as it moves through the tunnel. Engineers work out how long the roof and walls of the tunnel can stand up as the soil and rocks around them are removed.

Monster moles

The tunnel-boring machine is controlled by a team of 50 people, including three pilots who guide it using a computer and laser beams. The laser beams are fired along the tunnel, giving the mole a straight line to follow. The cutting head is pushed forwards by hydraulic rams. The rest of the tube can be between 328 and 820 feet (100–250 m) long, and supports the roof and walls of the tunnel.

How the mole digs

As the mole cuts through the ground, the **spoil** falls through holes in the cutting head. It is carried on a conveyor belt to trucks or railroad wagons that carry it out of the tunnel. In the Channel Tunnel, the spoil was turned into a liquid and carried to the top of the shafts in big pipes. A mole can dig in one day what it would take a person two months to dig!

This is how a mole, or T.B.M., digs and lines a tunnel and removes spoil. If all the soil and rock from the Channel Tunnel was piled up, it would be as tall as the Eiffel Tower.

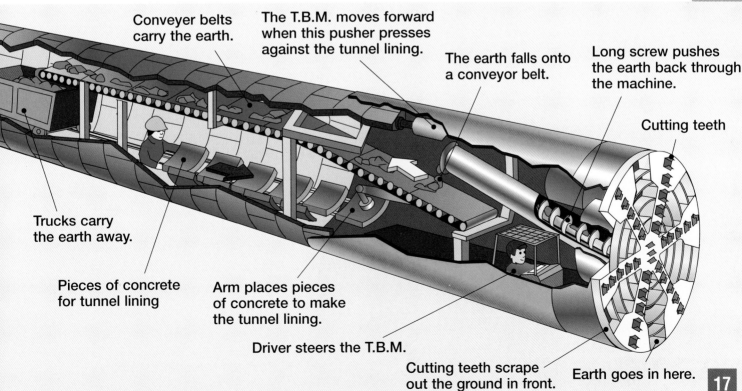

Conveyer belts carry the earth.

The T.B.M. moves forward when this pusher presses against the tunnel lining.

The earth falls onto a conveyor belt.

Long screw pushes the earth back through the machine.

Cutting teeth

Trucks carry the earth away.

Pieces of concrete for tunnel lining

Arm places pieces of concrete to make the tunnel lining.

Driver steers the T.B.M.

Cutting teeth scrape out the ground in front.

Earth goes in here.

17

Linings

Pieces of concrete lining travel along a rail towards the front of the mole, where an arm swings out and places each piece on the tunnel wall. Two factories, one in England and the other in France, made 720,000 reinforced concrete pieces to line the Channel Tunnel. They were stored for 10 days to let the concrete reach maximum strength. The joins between the pieces were sealed with special waterproof cement.

▲ **This piece of concrete has been molded for the lining of the Channel Tunnel.**

Tunneling under the river Thames

Early soft-ground tunneling was almost impossible until a man named Marc Isambard Brunel invented a tunneling shield to protect tunnelers from cave-ins and floods. The shield was a giant iron box which could be pushed forward through the soft, gooey soil beneath the river. Tunnelers worked from 36 cells inside the box facing a wall of removable planks of wood. Each tunneler removed one plank at a time, scooped out the soil, and quickly replaced the plank. While the shield held the gooey soil in place, bricklayers lined the tunnel walls with brick. Brunel got the idea for the shield from watching a tiny sea creature called a shipworm boring through wood, pushing the sawdust out behind it to make a smooth lining to the hole. It is easy to see where the idea for the modern mole came from.

◄ **Brunel's tunneling shield**

Building rock tunnels

The ancient Romans tunneled through solid rock by heating the rock face with fire and pouring cold water on it to crack the rock. Today, tunnels are driven through solid rock by shattering the rock into smaller pieces with explosives.

Master blasters

Blasting is much safer and more efficient now than when it was first tried on the Hoosac Tunnel, in Massachusetts, in the late 1800s. The Hoosac tunnelers used gunpowder and nitroglycerine, which were very difficult and dangerous explosives to handle. Hundreds of workers died in unexpected explosions.

Today, explosives are placed into several deep holes drilled into the tunnel face. The drill is powered by air and mounted on a vehicle called a jumbo. The explosives are carefully positioned so that the blast breaks the rock up in the right way. When everyone is a safe distance away, the powerful charges are **detonated**.

◄ Drilling holes for explosives in a water-supply tunnel in New York, 1988

Mucking

A small digging machine with a scoop collects the spoil and empties it onto a conveyor belt, which carries it to waiting railroad wagons or trucks. This is called mucking. The jumbo is moved back into place and more holes are drilled. In very hard rock, the tunnel might grow by 65 feet (20 m) a day. Fumes and dust created by the explosions are pumped out of the tunnel by fans. In some tunnels, a machine sprays a mist of water to make the dust settle quickly on the ground.

KEY WORDS

detonated made to explode

Lining

The solid walls and roof of a new rock tunnel support themselves. But blasting can weaken the rock, so metal arches are used as temporary supports, with strong wire netting to stop smaller chunks of rock from falling into the tunnel.

Blasting always leaves the tunnel walls and roof jagged. A smooth concrete lining is added later. Wooden or steel molds, called formwork, are placed around the tunnel. Concrete is then pumped behind the formwork. When the concrete has hardened, the formwork is removed, leaving a smooth surface.

Building canal tunnels

Before there were railroads and highways, canals were the cheapest and most reliable form of transportation. A canal needs to be as level as possible, so whenever a large hill was in the way of a new canal, digging a tunnel was the only answer. Canal tunnels built in the 1800s were dug by miners. They used only hammers, **picks**, and shovels to carve the tunnel out of solid rock. Spoil was loaded into baskets and carried out to waiting carts pulled by horses or donkeys. Tunneling was slow—only 12 feet (3.6 m) a week was dug.

Bricklayers followed, lining the walls with bricks. The 51-mile-long (83-km) underground canal system in Lancashire, England, is lined with six million bricks! This is the longest underground canal system in the world.

Most canal tunnels had low roofs. The boatmen would lie on their backs and "leg" their boats through by pushing their feet against the tunnel wall. Some tunnels had chains fixed to the wall for the boatmen to pull themselves along.

The Worsley canal system, in Lancashire, England, is the longest underground canal system in the world. ▶

KEY WORDS

picks tools for breaking up rock

Building cut-and-cover tunnels

Cut-and-cover tunnels are designed for tunnels being built close to the surface. The depth of the trench will depend on whether it is to be used by pedestrians and traffic or whether the tunnel is to carry services such as electricity and communications cables, gas, or water pipes.

Digging and lining

The trench for a cut-and-cover tunnel is dug along the route of the tunnel. A tunnel-boring machine is used for deeper tunnels and smaller digging machines for tunnels that will carry pipes closer to the surface. The tunnel walls are lined with reinforced concrete. The concrete might be poured or pumped into formwork at the site, or the tunnel linings might be made at a factory and brought to the site, where cranes will lift them into place.

Cut-and-cover tunnels are cheaper and faster to build, which makes them an ideal tunnel for busy areas. When the tunnel is completed, the soil and rocks that were removed are put back. The road surface is then laid, or, if it is an unpopulated area, the land is replanted with the grasses, trees, and shrubs that would normally be found there.

A ready-made section of a cut-and-cover tunnel, ready to be installed ▼

Building underwater tunnels

Most early underwater tunnels were built using a tunneling shield similar to the one used to dig the Thames Tunnel. Air was blasted into the shield so hard and fast that the water could not flow against it. If you make a small puddle of water on a flat surface and then blow steadily on the edge of the puddle, what happens to the water? This is how the air kept the water away from the tunnel face. The newest underwater tunnels are called immersed-tube tunnels. These tunnels lie on the sea- or river-bed rather than going through it.

To build an underwater tunnel, a trench is first dug along the sea- or river-bed for the tunnel to sit in. The tunnel arrives in ready-made sections, with each end of the hollow tubes plugged so that they float. Tugboats move each tunnel section into position. The sections are sunk and then joined together by divers to make a long tube that lies on the river- or sea-bed. The tunnel is weighted down with tons of concrete, and covered with gravel. The ends of the tubes are unplugged and the tunnel section pumped out. The lining is then added. Underwater tunnels must be extremely strong to withstand the weight of the water pressing against them. In water 164 feet (50 m) deep, the pressing is the same as if a huge truck was resting on every part of the tunnel.

Sections of an immersed-tube tunnel are floated and moved into position by tugboats. ▼

Building aqueducts

An aqueduct is a tunnel that carries water. Aqueducts bring fresh drinking water to our faucets, take dirty wastewater to where it can be cleaned, and remove stormwater from the streets to prevent flooding during heavy rain.

The longest tunnel in the world does not carry trains or cars—it carries water. The Delaware Aqueduct, in New York, is 104 miles (169 km) long and is part of the New York City water supply. The New York Third Water Tunnel is expected to be finished in 2020. It will be 60 miles (96 km) long and will deliver 1.1 billion gallons (4.9 billion l) of water to nine million people every day.

Laying pipes to carry water ▶

Some aqueducts carry water from a dam to a **hydro-electric power station**. The water is forced through giant waterwheels, called turbines, to make electricity. Another set of tunnels returns the water to the dam. The Snowy Mountains Hydro-electric Scheme, in Australia, is the largest in the world. It has 16 dams and seven power stations connected by 90 miles (145 km) of tunnels.

Building micro-tunnels

Tunnels for small pipes and drains are called micro-tunnels. Some micro-tunnels are dug by a machine called a remote-controlled drill. The drill is on a long, bendable pipe and is steered from a cabin on the ground above it. Sometimes, sections of ready-made pipe can be pushed through soft ground. This is called pipe-jacking. Pipe-jacking is useful when a narrow tunnel needs to pass beneath a major road or railroad, because there is no disruption to traffic or trains.

KEY WORDS

hydro-electric power station a power station that uses moving water to make electricity

WORKING TUNNELS

After a tunnel is built, it is prepared for use. All the spoil and equipment is removed from the site. Sometimes it is easier to leave the moles there. After the Channel Tunnel was finished, the 11 moles were too big to bring back through the lined tunnel. Some of them were taken apart and others were buried.

Finishing touches

In transportation tunnels, the road surface or railroad track is laid. Lighting, electricity, and water are installed. Speed signs and warning signs are posted throughout the tunnel so that people know what to do if there is an emergency such as a fire or a crash. In very long tunnels, sprinklers, fire extinguishers, and emergency telephones are installed. Watertight doors are fitted to seal off sections during flooding, and fireproof doors are put in place. Ventilation is extremely important. Fans and air ducts are installed to remove poisonous exhaust fumes and circulate fresh air. In a tunnel as big as the Channel Tunnel, emergency workers are on duty all the time.

In the Channel Tunnel, there is a smaller tunnel running between the two larger tunnels. This tunnel is used by **maintenance** crews and as an escape route during an emergency.

Wildlife tunnels

Some freeways run through wildlife areas. Many animals are killed or injured trying to cross such wide, busy roads. Tunnels have been built under some freeways to help the animals cross safely. Where a dam blocks a river, water-filled tunnels allow fish to swim around the dam and into the river further down. This type of tunnel is called a fish ladder.

KEY WORDS

maintenance keeping something in good condition

Looking after tunnels

Tunnels need to be checked regularly for signs of cracking and leaking. Emergency equipment is tested and anything that must be replaced or repaired is done so immediately.

Mining tunnels

The tunneling in mining tunnels does not stop until the mine is emptied of all its minerals or precious metals. Depending on what is being mined, mining tunnels are blasted, drilled, or dug by massive cutting machines. Some shafts are deeper than 1,900 feet (600 m).

The mine is like a small town, with offices, workshops, and a cafeteria. Small trains drive the miners to and from the part of the mine that is being worked. Mining is as dangerous as any other type of tunneling. There is always a risk of cave-ins, poisonous gases, explosion and fire, and flooding. Sometimes the miners freeze the underground water before digging to prevent flooding. In early mines, miners took caged birds with them. If the bird died, it meant poisonous gases were present.

Escape tunnels

Escape tunnels are used in some countries where people live close to an erupting volcano. The tunnels are strong arches built of clear material above ground, allowing people to move to safety as soon as an eruption begins. The tunnels' tough material resists the heat of lava. It protects people from poisonous gases and pieces of rock as big as cars, which can be hurled out by the volcano.

An avalanche shelter on a railroad line in Switzerland ▼

TUNNELS THAT WENT WRONG

In the past, some tunnels went wrong because engineers did not understand how to make structures strong and stable. There were no computers or tests that could tell them if the ground was solid enough to support a structure or if there were weaknesses in the tunnel design.

Building problems

Unexpected problems and accidents can occur during the building of a tunnel.

Lötschberg Tunnel

In 1908, water and gravel gushed into the Lötschberg Tunnel under the Swiss Alps. One mile (more than 1 km) was filled with water, gravel, and spoil, and 25 tunnelers were killed. The tunnelers thought they were digging into bedrock, but they had hit the soft ground beneath a river.

Simplon railroad tunnel

The Simplon railroad tunnel reaches more than 6,564 feet (2,000 m) into Earth's crust under the Alps between Italy and Switzerland. At this depth, underground water can almost boil. During tunneling, scalding-hot water poured into the digging site. To be able to continue building the tunnel, ice-cold water had to be pumped into the tunnel and sprayed onto the rock to cool it down.

◀ In 1828, water surged into the tunnel face of the Thames Tunnel, London, killing six tunnelers.

Athens Metro, Greece

A news reporter was sent to a street in Athens, Greece, to report on a suspicious rumbling sound and some mysteriously moving paving stones. The reporter was interviewing the owner of a nearby newsstand, when it collapsed and disappeared into a hole that had suddenly opened up in the pavement. Looking into the hole, the reporter could see the spinning head of a tunnel-boring machine!

Accidents and natural disasters

An unexpected flood or earthquake can severely damage a tunnel. Accidents that happen inside the tunnel may not damage the tunnel itself, but can still cause death and injury to the people inside.

Fire

One of the worst things that can happen in a long tunnel is a fire. The Channel Tunnel has an emergency tunnel running through it so that people can escape if a fire breaks out. Not all tunnels have this. In October 2001, two trucks collided in the Saint Gotthard road tunnel, in Switzerland, bursting into flames. Eleven people died because the smoke from the fire was spread through the tunnel by the ventilation system. Fierce heat caused part of the arched roof to collapse, trapping many people. The fire was still burning 24 hours after the accident.

Mont Blanc Tunnel

When a truck caught fire in the Mont Blanc Tunnel, in March 1999, dozens of vehicles came to a stop in the tunnel. At least 39 people died in the fire from breathing poisonous fumes. It took two days to put out the fire. Extra air was pumped into the tunnel to help trapped people breathe, but it just made the fire hotter and fiercer.

Emergency crews arrive at the Mont Blanc Tunnel fire in 1999. ▼

AMAZING TUNNELS

Some of the world's most amazing structures are tunnels. Some tunnels are record-breakers because of their length or their design. Other tunnels are famous because they were the first to use certain building materials or because ways of solving difficult problems were found during their building. Here are some interesting facts and figures—there are many more you can find out about.

The world's longest rail tunnel

The Seikan Tunnel, in Japan, is the longest rail tunnel and the longest and deepest underwater tunnel in the world. The tunnel is 33 miles (54 km) in length, with 14 miles (22.5 km) running beneath Japan's Tsugaru Strait. The tunnel is as high as a three-story building and is 800 feet (243 m) below the sea. It was built after a violent storm with huge waves sank five ferry boats in 1954, killing 1,430 people.

◀ **The Seikan Tunnel, Japan**

Engineers could not use a tunnel-boring machine to dig the Seikan Tunnel, because the ground was unstable. Instead, they blasted and drilled 33 miles (53 km) through a major earthquake zone! More than 3,137 tons (2,845 t) of explosives and 188,184 tons (170,688 t) of steel were used. More than 21,000 concrete slabs were used for the railroad track. If you stacked them one on top of the other, they would be nearly twice the height of Japan's Mount Fuji.

The tunnel flooded four times. In 1976, soft rock collapsed. So much water gushed into the tunnel that it took more than two months to control the flood. Luckily, no lives were lost. The tunnel opened in 1988—42 years after work first began.

Tunnel world records

- Longest tunnel: Delaware Aqueduct, New York. Water supply tunnel completed in 1965. Length: 104 miles (169 km).
- Deepest tunnel: Hitra Tunnel, Norway. Road tunnel completed in 1994. Depth: 866 feet (264 m) below sea level.
- Biggest tunnel: Yerba Tunnel, San Francisco Bay, California. Road tunnel completed in 1936. Width: 78 feet (24 m). Height: 55 feet (17 m).

Tunneling firsts

- First rail tunnel: The Mont Cenis Tunnel running between France and Italy began in 1857, and was completed in 1871. It was eight miles (13 km) long—three times longer than any tunnel before it. It was also the first time dynamite was used to blast through rock.
- The first use of air-powered drills and high explosives such as nitroglycerine was in the Hoosac Tunnel, Massachusetts. The tunnel was completed in 1873. It is 4.75 miles (7.6 km) long.
- First use of electric fans for ventilation in a tunnel: The Holland Tunnel, in New York City, was the first long underwater road tunnel in the world. Completed in 1927, the tunnel runs under the Hudson River. It has four massive towers at both ends of the tunnel, which house 84 powerful electric fans. Each fan is 80 feet (24 m) in diameter.

▼ **The Holland Tunnel**

USING MODELS TO LEARN ABOUT STRUCTURES

You can find out about some of the challenges engineers meet when they design and build a tunnel by using a construction set to build your own. Construction sets have all the important building parts that you can use to make supports and linings. You can even test out different tunnel shapes.

Strength and stability are just as important in a construction set as they are in a life-sized structure. Many of today's engineers and architects started with construction sets. They are still building with them—the construction sets just grew bigger.

Construction sets are a great way to learn about strong and stable tunnels. ▼

GLOSSARY

alloy	a mixture of two or more metals
avalanche shelters	tunnels that protect a mountain road or railroad from being buried beneath moving snow and ice
bracing	something fastened to an object to keep it stiff and straight, just like the braces worn on teeth
braziers	metal containers in which a fire can be burned
canals	waterways made by humans
cement	an ingredient in concrete which makes the concrete harden like stone
concrete	a building material made by mixing cement and sand or gravel with water
detonated	made to explode
engineers	people who design and build large structures
excavation	digging
geologists	scientists who study soil and rocks
hydraulic	works by using water or another liquid under pressure
hydro-electric power station	a power station that uses moving water to make electricity
lava shelters	tunnels that people can escape through when a nearby volcano erupts
maintenance	keeping something in good condition
materials	anything used to make a structure
picks	tools for breaking up rock
prairie dog	a small, furry animal like a ground squirrel or possum which lives underground in large groups
reinforced	made stronger
sewers	channels that carry sewage to where it can be treated
shafts	vertical passages or tunnels
spoil	rock or soil dug from a tunnel face
structure	something that is made up of many parts joined together
temporary	for a short time only
termites	ant-like insects
tunnel face	the area at the end of the tunnel that is being dug

INDEX